Dear Reader,

It is so cool that you like to read!

Elephant and Piggie like to read too. So, I thought I would share some of their favorite books with you!

In *The Monster and Puppet Show!*, Puppet asks Monster for more and MORE! What should Monster do when too much more is no fun anymore?

I hope you enjoy this story as much as Elephant and Piggie do!

Your pal,

Mo!

"What do you call a sleeping dinosaur?"

"I do not know."

"What *do* you call a sleeping dinosaur?"

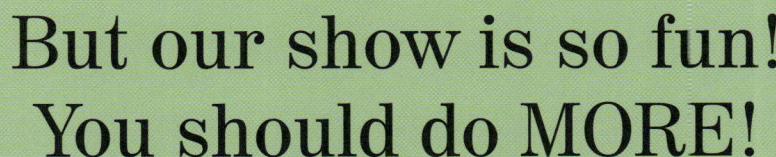

To Mo for believing in me.
To Tracey for joyfully leading the way.
And to Mikey for always saving the day!
—K.M.

UNION SQUARE KIDS and the distinctive Union Square Kids logo are trademarks of Hachette Book Group, Inc.

Text and illustrations © 2026 Kate Micucci

ELEPHANT & PIGGIE text and illustrations © 2026 Hidden Pigeon, LLC. ELEPHANT & PIGGIE characters and related elements are trademarks of Hidden Pigeon, LLC.

All rights reserved. No part of this publication may be reproduced, stored in a retrieval system, or transmitted in any form or by any means (including electronic, mechanical, photocopying, recording, or otherwise) without prior written permission from the publisher.

Union Square Kids books may be purchased in bulk for business, educational, or promotional use. For more information, please contact your local bookseller or the Hachette Book Group's Special Markets department at special.markets@hbgusa.com.

HC ISBN: 9781454951476

Printed in China.

Lot #:
10 9 8 7 6 5 4 3 2 1
10/25

unionsquareandco.com
HiddenPigeonCompany.com

Design by James Protano and Amelia Mack.

This book is set in Century725 BT, Bananas VF, Billy, Futura, and Avenir LT.

Library of Congress Control Number: 2025023372

# ELEPHANT & PIGGIE also like reading:

**The Cookie Fiasco**
by Dan Santat

**We Are Growing!**
by Laurie Keller
(Theodor Seuss Geisel Medal)

**The Good for Nothing Button!**
by Charise Mericle Harper

**It's Shoe Time!**
by Bryan Collier

**The Itchy Book!**
by LeUyen Pham

**Harold & Hog Pretend for Real!**
by Dan Santat

**What About Worms!?**
by Ryan T. Higgins
(Theodor Seuss Geisel Honor)

**I'm On It!**
by Andrea Tsurumi

**It's a Sign!**
by Jarrett Pumphrey
and Jerome Pumphrey